BOYS RULE!

Mega Rich

Felice Arena and Phil Kettle

illustrated by
Gus Gordon

RISING ★ STARS

First Published in Great Britain by
RISING STARS UK LTD 2006
22 Grafton Street, London, W1S 4EX

For more information visit our website at:
www.risingstars-uk.com

British Library Cataloguing in Publication Data
A CIP record for this book is available from the British Library.

ISBN: 978-1-84680-058-0

First published in 2006 by
MACMILLAN EDUCATION AUSTRALIA PTY LTD
627 Chapel Street, South Yarra 3141

Visit our website at www.macmillan.com.au or
go directly to www.macmillanlibrary.com.au

Associated companies and representatives throughout the world.

Series created by Felice Arena and Phil Kettle
Project management by Limelight Press Pty Ltd
Cover and text design by Lore Foye
Illustrations by Gus Gordon

Printed in China

UK Editorial by Westcote Computing Editorial Services

Contents

Billy   Sam

CHAPTER 1

A Fratillionaire

It's the summer holidays and best
friends Billy and Sam are spending
time together at Billy's house. The boys
are flicking through a bike magazine.

Sam "Wow! Look at that! That's so cool."

Billy "Yes, that's the Mountain Rally 3000."

Sam "I think that's the closest thing to riding a rocket."

Billy "Brilliant!"

Sam "How much does it cost?"

Billy quickly flips the page over to read the price.

Billy and Sam "Wow!"
Billy "Three thousand pounds."
Sam "For a bike? You can buy a car for that much."

Billy "Or a million burgers."

Sam "Three thousand pounds would be nothing if you were mega rich, like a billionaire or something."

Billy "Yes. I want to be a billionaire. My whole house would be made out of gold bricks."

Sam "Right, well I want to be a gazillionaire."

Billy "Or a squillionaire."

Sam "Or a fratillionaire."

Billy "A what? You just made that up."

Sam "Yes, I did. But wouldn't it be cool to buy anything you want?"

Billy "Hey, I've got an idea."

Sam "What?"

Billy "I know how we can make
   heaps of money. Right now!"

Sam "Cool! So then we can become
   mega rich! But how are we going to
   do it?"

Billy "Follow me."

Sam follows Billy into the kitchen.

CHAPTER 2

Squeeze and Sell

Billy and Sam are standing in the kitchen cutting up oranges. They start squeezing the juice into two large jugs.

Sam "This is a great idea. Make our own juice and sell it."

Billy "I know. It's the best idea ever. Keep squeezing."

The boys fill the jugs right up to the top. Billy adds sugar and ice cubes to both jugs.

Billy "Right, now we're ready for business."

Sam "Cool! We're going to be mega rich. Everyone loves juice."

The boys set up a folding table on the pavement in front of Billy's house and place the jugs on it.

Sam "Hang on, we need cups."
Billy "Right, I'll be back."

Billy rushes inside and returns
with some plastic cups and a sign.

Sam "What's that?"
Billy "We need a sign to let people
know what we're selling."

Sam "Cool!"

Billy tapes the paper sign onto the front of the table. It reads "Cool juice 4 sale. Only 50p a cup!".

Billy "Now all we've got to do is wait for the people to come."
Sam "And the money!"

CHAPTER 3

Take That!

The boys wait. Minutes pass and
no one appears.

Sam "Cor, it's hot!"

Billy "Yes, it is. And I'm getting
really thirsty."

Sam "Me too! That juice really is looking good. Do you think I could have one drink?"

Billy "Why not? I'll have one too."

The boys pour themselves a cup of juice each.

Billy "Mmmm, that's great juice. We did a pretty good job."

COOL
JUICE 4
SaLe

Sam "Yes. We're great juice makers. Can I have another one?"

Billy "Er, yes, OK. I think I'll have another one too."

Billy sucks on some ice cubes, then he suddenly spits one down the back of Sam's neck.

Sam "Hey! What are you doing?"

Billy (laughing) "Just trying to cool you off."

Sam "Yes, well maybe *you* need cooling off."

Sam grabs an ice cube from his cup and shoves it down the front of Billy's T-shirt.

Billy scoops up a cup of orange juice and throws it over Sam's head. Sam picks up the jug.

Sam "This means war!"
Billy "Bring it on!"

Within moments the boys are in the middle of an all-out juice fight.

Billy "Take that!"

Sam "Yes? Well, take this!"

Splash! Splosh! Splash!

The juice fight ends when, suddenly, a lady appears wanting to buy a cold drink. Billy and Sam look at each other in shock. The jugs are empty!

CHAPTER 4

The Performers

The lady walks off down the street,
disappointed that Billy and Sam have
splashed away all the juice.

Billy "Oh no! What a waste. We missed our chance. We could have made some money then."

Sam "I know. Quick, let's go and squeeze some more oranges."

Billy "We can't. We used them all up."

Sam "Let's go and buy some then."

Billy "We can't. We don't have any money. That's the problem."

Sam "So how can we get mega rich if we haven't got any money to use?"

Billy "I've got another great idea. Just wait here for a moment."

Billy runs indoors and returns a few minutes later with three tennis balls and a harmonica.

Sam "What's all that for?"

Billy "Didn't you tell me once that you can juggle?"

Sam "Yes, sort of."

Billy hands the tennis balls to Sam.

Billy "Then you juggle and I'll play the harmonica."

Sam "I didn't know you could play the harmonica."

Billy "Yes, but only one song—'Row, Row, Row Your Boat'. OK, you juggle and I'll play."

Billy places his cap on the ground.

Sam "What are you doing that for?"

Billy "We'll be street performers.
Like the ones I've seen in town!
They make heaps of money. People
just *throw* money at their feet."

Sam "Oh yes, I've seen them. Right, so *that's* what we're doing with your cap. So everyone can throw money in it for us."

Billy "OK. Let's start performing."

CHAPTER 5

The Law Steps In

Billy and Sam begin their
"performance". Billy's harmonica
playing sounds out of tune and Sam
struggles to juggle three balls at a
time. After a minute or so they stop.

Billy "Maybe we should wait until we have an audience."

Sam "Yes, that's what I think, too."

Billy "If we do this every day for a week, we're going to make heaps."

Sam "Cool!"

Billy "When I'm rich, I'm going to pay a jet fighter pilot to fly me up in his jet so I can parachute into school."

Sam "Great. I'm going to give all my money away to animal hospitals so they can help ill dogs, cats, birds, tigers and hedgehogs."

Billy "What? All of it? You wouldn't keep any for yourself?"

Sam "Well, maybe enough to buy that Mountain Rally 3000 bike."

Billy shakes his head in disbelief.

Billy "It's your money I suppose.

Billy starts making strange noises.

Sam "What are you doing?"
Billy "I'm singing! Mum plays this
song in the car all the time. It goes
like this …"

Sam "Er, maybe you should save it for the performance."

Billy "As if I could sing with a harmonica in my mouth."

Sam "Now that would be cool! Look, someone's coming! Stop singing and start playing."

Billy plays his harmonica and Sam juggles while the person approaches.

Sam "Hey, it's a policeman."
Billy "He doesn't look very happy."

The policeman tells Sam and Billy that they can't perform unless they have a special licence. They don't, so they have to stop.

Billy "Well, that stinks!"

Sam "Yes, what are we going to do now?"

Billy "I don't know."

Sam "Do you want to go and play football in the park?"

Billy "How's that going to make us any cash?"

Sam "It's not. We'll have to get mega rich another day."

Billy thinks for a second.

Billy "Yes. Good idea. It takes too much hard work to make money."

BOYS RULE!

Money Lingo

Sam   Billy

bank A safe place where most people keep their money. Others keep it in secret hiding spots—so secret that even they can't remember where it is!

cash Another way of saying money when you mean notes and coins.

entrepreneur Someone who comes up with business ideas to make money. Someone like the man who was first to invent bubble gum ... or even Billy!

rich When you have lots of money. You know you're rich when you've got your own helicopter in your garden.

BOYS RULE!
Money Must-dos

☞ When you're sitting in the back seat of your parents' car and you want to feel like you've got lots of money, say, "Driver, take me home please".

☞ If you have any good ideas about how to make money, write them down or draw them in a book. But make sure your sister doesn't find it because she'll probably end up making a fortune out of them.

☞ A good way to annoy your sister and perhaps make a little money at the same time is ask your parents if you can sell her on eBay.

☞ To learn more about money, watch TV game shows and try to answer the questions. See how much you'd win!

☞ If you ever become mega rich, find out how you can help other people—except for your sister of course!

☞ If you want to find some cash, try looking behind the cushions on the couch or in the bottom of your school bag.

BOYS RULE!
Money
Instant Info

 JK Rowling, the author of the "Harry Potter" books, is one of the richest women in the world. She has more money than the Queen.

 The owner of Microsoft, Bill Gates, is one of the richest men in the world. He has £21 billion ... he could probably buy the Moon for that much and still have some change left over!

 Wembley Stadium cost £757 million to build. No wonder it's one of the best buildings in the world.

One of the most expensive paintings in the world is a painting by an artist called Pablo Picasso. It's worth more than 100 million American dollars. So, keep all your drawings—you just never know.

 Money in Italy, France and Germany is called the euro. In Japan it's called the yen.

BOYS RULE!

Think Tank

1 What's the best type of juice to use in a juice fight?

2 Is a Mountain Rally 3000 bike for riding in the mountains or on a cycle path?

3 If you tried to buy four cups of juice from Billy and Sam, how much would it cost in total? (trick question)

4 What word rhymes with "money" and describes the Boys Rule! stories?

5 Where would you see a street performer perform?

6 Who plays the harmonica—badly?

7 What two things do you need to be a street performer?

8 Name one thing that's just as good or even better than making money?

Answers

The answers below are printed upside down:

1 Any type of juice is good for a juice fight, as long as it's wet!

2 The Mountain Rally 3000 is excellent for riding in the mountains and on cycle paths. So whichever one you answered, you're right.

3 The total would be zero because there's no juice left.

4 "Funny" rhymes with "money" and describes the "Boys Rule!" stories.

5 Street performers perform on the street, of course!

6 Billy plays the harmonica.

7 You need a licence to be a street performer—and a really good act.

8 Playing football with your best friend is just as good as making money.

How did you score?

- If you got all 8 answers correct, then you love money. You have a million ideas on how to become mega rich, just like Billy and Sam.

- If you got 6 answers correct, then you know how to spend money—and you probably have your own wallet.

- If you got fewer than 4 answers correct, then you probably like money, but don't worry too much about making it—at least not yet.

Felice → ← Phil

Hi Guys!

We have heaps of fun reading and want you to, too. We both believe that being a good reader is really important and so cool.

Try out our suggestions to help you have fun as you read.

At school, why don't you use "Mega Rich" as a play and you and your friends can be the actors. Set the scene for your play. Bring some jugs and cups to school to use as props! Or borrow a harmonica and practise playing it. Maybe someone in the class can actually juggle!

So ... have you decided who is going to be Billy and who is going to be Sam? Now, with your friends, read and act out our story in front of the class.

We have a lot of fun when we go to schools and read our stories. After we finish the children all clap really loudly. When you've finished your play your classmates will do the same. Just remember to look out the window—there might be a talent scout from a television channel watching you!

Reading at home is really important and a lot of fun as well.

Take our books home and get someone in your family to read them with you. Maybe they can take on a part in the story.

Remember, reading is fun.

So, as the frog in the local pond would say, Read-it!

And remember, Boys Rule!

BOYS RULE!

When We Were Kids

Felice

Phil

Phil "Did you ever have a piggy bank when you were a kid?"

Felice "No. I had an old suitcase."

Phil "A suitcase?"

Felice "Yes. I put all my loose change in it and I finally filled it last week."

Phil "Really, how much did you save?"

Felice "Two thousand pounds and seven pence."

Phil "Wow! What are you going to buy?"

Felice "Heaps of 'Boys Rule!' books."

What a Laugh!

Q What kind of money do fishermen make?

A Net profits.

BOYS RULE!

 Gone Fishing

 The Tree House

 Golf Legends

 Camping Out

 Bike Daredevils

 Water Rats

 Skateboard Dudes

 Tennis Ace

 Basketball Buddies

 Secret Agent Heroes

Wet World

Rock Star

Pirate Attack

Olympic Champions

 Race Car Dreamers

 Hit the Beach

Rotten School Day

Halloween Gotcha!

Battle of the Games

 On the Farm